TALES FROM HALLOWEENTOWN

The Witch's Amulet

By Lucy Ruggles

Based on "Halloweentown," Written by Paul Bernbaum

New York

Library of Congress Catalog Card Number: 2007922748

ISBN-13: 978 1-4231-0881-8
ISBN-10: 1-4231-0881-7
For more Disney Press fun, visit www.disneybooks.com
Visit DisneyChannel.com

CHAPTER
ONE

Marnie Piper threw open the stained glass window of her dorm room, relieved that she had survived her first year at Witch University.

After the headache of exams in Egyptian Pyramidology, Beginning Welsh for Spells, Introduction to Rituals, and Calculus 101, Marnie was ready for a break—a nice, long summer break with no studying, no tests, and no brother always hanging around to bug her. Dylan would be too busy with his summer job as a lab assistant to cause her problems. He was helping Professor

Lucius La Biel at the University Research Center for Magical Science. Just one more example, in his older sister's astute opinion, that Dylan was your classic overachiever.

Marnie was interrupted by a knock at her door. "Come in," she called, tucking a stray strand of blond hair behind her ear. Aneesa appeared suddenly in her room, her arms crossed in front of her and her long, brown ponytail swinging.

"I thought genies could only nod themselves into their lamps," said Marnie suspiciously.

"Maybe your average genie," Aneesa winked, "but I've been learning a few new tricks." She plopped herself down on Marnie's big, pillow-covered canopy bed. "So how's your first day on the job?"

As Marnie's friend and former Resident Advisor, Aneesa had helped her get a summer gig as RA of the girl's dorm for Witch U.'s Summer Sorcery School. Young witches and warlocks came from all around to get extra practice with their magic, and the campus was swarming with the newly arrived high school students. It was the resident advisors' job to keep things running smoothly and keep their young charges happy and safe. Marnie knew all too well that where witches gathered, trouble often followed.

"It's going great!" assured Marnie. "It makes me feel all warm and fuzzy to know I'm doing my part to help shape the bright, young magical minds of tomorrow."

"You haven't met any of your advisees yet, have you?" Aneesa asked.

"Nope."

The two girls giggled. There was another knock at the door.

"Ah, my first bright, young mind!" Marnie said, smiling at Aneesa.

She pointed a finger at the heavy wooden door and it creaked open. But instead of an eager, young witch seeking Marnie's advice, there stood Sophie, Marnie's younger sister.

Back from her tour of the worlds (chaperoned, of course, by Grandma Aggie), Sophie had been allowed to enroll at summer school only because

Marnie would be there to look after her. The task was unwelcome on both sides. Marnie didn't want to be her sister's keeper for the summer any more than Sophie wanted a babysitter.

"Hi, Soph," Marnie said, slightly surprised to see her so soon.

Marnie had figured Sophie would be too busy with her best friends, Stephanie and Sylvie ("the sidekicks," as Dylan called them) to acknowledge her older sister's existence. But apparently she had been wrong. Stephanie and Sylvie stood behind Sophie at the door now.

"Hey," Sophie said in an annoyed tone of voice.

"What's up?" Marnie asked.

"We need to know where the auditorium is." Sophie held up her schedule as evidence. On the piece of paper was a picture of a clock, only where each number should have been, there was a streaming video of what the students would be doing at that time. "We have something called 'ori-enta-lation' in an hour."

"Orientation," Marnie corrected.

"Whatever," Sophie sighed. "Can you tell us how to get there?"

"Don't you have a map?" wondered Marnie.

"No."

"That's weird. You should have gotten one," she said, trying not to lose her cool with her sister, who she knew was just trying to impress her friends. "Come on in. I think I have extras."

The three girls stepped into Marnie's room. Stephanie and Sylvie looked around, assessing the room: Marnie's king-size bed; the medieval tapestry—a gift from her grandmother—which hung on the wall; the tall bookshelf, which reached all the way up to the ceiling, holding spell books, notebooks, and textbooks; her desk with both a computer and the quill pen she used in calligraphy class.

Marnie searched through the clutter of her desk drawers until she pulled out a stack of papers. She handed a map to each of the girls. "It'll change direction with you, so you can see where you're going," she explained.

They nodded, turning around in circles to see the map orient itself, like a compass.

There was another knock at the door.

"Finally, your bright, young mind!" Aneesa teased.

Marnie laughed, opening the door. "I guess I should just leave it open!"

But they were wrong again. This time it was only Marnie's boyfriend, Ethan.

Marnie had lost touch with Ethan after her bumpy attempt to bring Halloweentown kids to her high school in the mortal world. But after reconnecting back in Halloweentown at Witch U., they'd become almost as inseparable as the conjoined twins in their class. Lucky for them, Ethan was overseeing the boys' dorm.

"Hey, Pumpkin?" Ethan asked now, his handsome face turning red under the weight of the huge, ancient-looking leather trunk he was carrying.

"Pumpkin?" Sophie repeated the pet name. Standing behind Marnie, she rolled her eyes.

"Could you help me with something?" Ethan's

legs were bending lower and lower to the ground. He was about to collapse under the weight of the trunk.

"Sure, Baby Boo. What?" Marnie asked.

"Maybe the four-*hundred*-pound trunk he's carrying?" Sophie said sarcastically. Marnie turned and shot her a warning look. "Just a guess."

Marnie waved her hand in a circle. "Cargo ligerum," she said quickly. Suddenly Ethan stood up straight, the strain falling from his face.

"Whew," he exhaled. "Thanks. Sophie, Aneesa," he acknowledged. "Sylvie, Stephanie."

"Hi," the sidekicks chimed in unison. They looked at Ethan with goo-goo eyes.

"What's in the trunk?" Marnie asked.

"Good question." Ethan lifted it now as if it were light as a feather. He shook it. From inside came the distinct *riiibbbit* of a frog and the mournful *baaaaaah* of a goat. A glittery substance sprinkled out of the trunk and onto Marnie's carpet. "One of my advisees needed help moving in. And I figured you could make it a tad easier for me, Pumpkin."

Everyone but Aneesa nodded their heads in understanding. "You witches are weird," she said.

"I'm not a witch anymore!" Ethan argued. "I gave up my powers, remember?"

Not too long ago, Ethan's dad had been stripped of his powers by the Halloweentown Council. So, Ethan had given up his powers as well, opting instead for the "uncomplicated" life of a human.

"Present company excluded then," Aneesa said, corrected.

"Thanks. Well, duty calls," Ethan said, ducking back out the door with the trunk. "We still going to that fly-in movie tonight?" he asked over his shoulder.

Marnie smiled. "I'll bring the broom. You bring the popcorn."

"Yuck," Sophie said, once Ethan was gone. "You guys are like Schmoopy-ville, population: 2."

"Yeah? Well, you will be, too, one day," Marnie warned ominously.

"Doubtful," Sophie assured her, cocking her

head and putting her hand on her hip. "We have to go. Stephanie wants to make sure her unicorn is okay at the stables." Sophie abruptly turned to leave, her sidekicks trailing behind her.

"Okay . . . bye!" Marnie called down the hall after them. "And don't forget we're going to see Mom off tomorrow!"

Marnie closed the door and sighed, sitting on the bed next to Aneesa.

"So, that was your sister?" Aneesa asked.

Marnie rolled her eyes. "Yep. Or so they tell me."

"That will be nice, having her around all summer."

Marnie looked doubtful. Had Aneesa just seen the same snooty teenager leave her room as she had? "We'll see. She can be a real pain in the butt. Sophie's a little strong-willed. I worry she might get herself into trouble."

A smile played on Aneesa's mouth. "Sounds like someone else I know."

"Watch it," Marnie laughed, tossing a pillow at her friend. "Or I might turn you into a goat."

CHAPTER TWO

The next day, on a different part of campus, Dylan Piper pulled a pair of large, protective plastic goggles down over his glasses. He had watched this experiment done a dozen times in science class, but still, he thought, one could never be too safe. There were rules to follow. One couldn't just experiment willy-nilly, throwing in a dash of butterfly-wing dust here or a drop of octopus tears there! Science was serious stuff.

Yes, Dylan was right at home here at the Witch University Research Center for Magical Science.

His crisp, white lab coat even felt like it was made for him. As he poured some crystal powder into a beaker of water and watched it bubble, the liquid turning first a deep red and then a bright shade of blue, he thought how lucky he was to be working under the instruction of Professor Lucius La Biel.

Dr. La Biel was one of Halloweentown's most prominent—and controversial—scientists and warlocks. His work on shape-shifting potions and levitation tonics had made him world-famous. The Halloweentown Council had even awarded him the city's prestigious Skeleton Key in gratitude for his service. But this latest project, the one on which Dylan was assisting for the summer, would be his greatest achievement yet. La Biel was on the brink of finding the formula for one of the most precious and elusive substances ever to be concocted in magical science: a youth serum.

Of course, La Biel had his doubters and his opponents. Many creatures in Halloweentown thought aging was something even witches should not tamper with, much like love. Still, La

Biel pressed on, determined. And now, Dylan would be right there to help him.

Lost in his thoughts, Dylan was startled when he heard a familiar voice behind him: "Hey, dude, what's up?"

Dylan turned. A fellow lab assistant named Fred was standing behind him, peering over Dylan's shoulder at the gurgling beaker. Fred was a tall, gangly scarecrow. While Dylan's lab coat came appropriately to his knees, Fred's hung just past his waist and looked like a sloppy, untucked shirt. Fred wasn't much for tucking in his shirts, anyway. A skateboarder, he liked to wear baggy cargo pants, sneakers, and a baseball cap that Professor La Biel insisted he take off in the lab.

Despite Fred's generally untidy appearance, Dylan liked him. They both liked science and math and could talk about books no one else had read. Dylan was excited to have found another "science nerd," and in the short week they'd been working in the lab, Dylan and Fred had struck up an easy friendship.

Dylan turned back to his beaker. "Just a simple crystallization reaction," he answered. "Professor La Biel needs it for the dinosaur-egg trials this afternoon."

"Man, you get to do all the cool stuff," complained Fred, leaning on the lab table. "All I ever get to do is clean test tubes." He kicked at the floor with his sneaker, which made a screeching sound on the clean tiles.

"Well, I have to wash test tubes, too," Dylan reminded him, pouring the blue gel from the beaker into five small tubes and taking them over to the incubator.

"Yeah," Fred said, following behind him, "but La Biel lets you help with the experiments, or at least prepare for them. Sometimes I wonder why he even gave me this job if all he's gonna do is make me clean up after him!"

"Well, someone has to," Dylan said, sliding the test-tube rack under the incubator's glowing orange lights.

The truth was, he knew, that Fred was a bit on

the clumsy side. His first day, Fred had managed to break two glass stirrers and knock over a beaker of bat venom.

"Not all science can be glamorous, Fred," Dylan went on. "If there weren't clean beakers and test tubes, none of these experiments could be done."

"Yeah, I guess so, man," Fred grumbled. Then his face brightened, his large mouth turning up into a smile. "Hey, what are you doing for lunch today? Wanna hit the skateboard course at All Hallow's Park? I can teach you a couple tricks."

Fred had been using lunch hours to teach Dylan skateboarding moves—or at least he'd been trying to. Dylan wasn't as good on wheels as he was in the lab. Still, Fred wasn't giving up on him. He assured Dylan that he'd also been a clumsy mess when he'd first learned. He'd even pulled up a pant leg to show Dylan his "battle wounds"—scabbed-over scrapes and scars on his knobby, scarecrow legs.

"I'd like to, but I have to go home for lunch today," said Dylan. "My mom's leaving for an extended vacation."

"Sweet. Where's she going?" asked Fred.

"Hawaii."

"Awesome! I hear they have major swells down there this time of year." Fred made the surfer's hang-ten sign, sticking out his thumb and pinky finger.

"Well, I doubt she'll be getting much surfing in," said Dylan. "My mom gets seasick in the bathtub. Hey," it occurred to him, "do you wanna come with me? My Grandma Aggie is making her famous chili."

"Thanks, dude. I can always eat some home cookin'." Fred grinned.

"Frreeedd," a goblin's voice called out from the laboratory's storage room. It was Dr. Rosenblumen, one of the scientists working with Professor La Biel on the youth serum.

"Yeeesss," Fred called in return, rolling his eyes.

"Vee haf a problem viz zee beakers. Zey haf zee spots." Dr. Rosenblumen was a stickler for cleanliness. "I vill need you to vash zem again."

Unseen by the scientist, Fred silently mimicked the small, hunched-over goblin's demand.

"Frreeedd? Did you hear me?" the doctor called again, louder this time.

"Yes, Dr. Rosenblumen. Spots. Coming!" Fred reluctantly walked toward the storage room, hanging his head dramatically. "See you at lunch?" he said to Dylan on his way out of the lab.

"Yaa," answered Dylan, going to check on his incubating test tubes. "Good luck viz zee beakers."

By the time Dylan and Fred made it back through the portal to Gwen's house in the mortal world, Marnie was already helping Aggie add the chili's final secret ingredient: a quarter-teaspoon of powdered mugwort. Gwen, meanwhile, was rushing through the house like a hurricane, making sure she hadn't forgotten anything for her trip.

"Where's Sophie?" Dylan asked, dipping a wooden spoon into the bubbling pot of chili.

Marnie shooed his hand away. "She had a clairvoyance class. She said she couldn't miss it."

"Speaking of class—Grandma, aren't you teaching one this summer?" Dylan asked.

Aggie brightened. "Why yes, I am! Professor Periwinkle and I teamed up for a course on time. But Dylan, enough about me. You have better manners than this. Introduce us to your tall friend!"

Since they had arrived, Fred had been standing silently behind Dylan, watching Marnie's every move. Now everyone turned to him, and he blushed when he was caught staring.

"Everyone, this is Fred. Fred, this is everyone," said Dylan, gesturing around the kitchen.

"Hey. I'm Fred." He quickly reached across the stove to shake Marnie's hand.

She laughed. "So I hear. I'm Marnie. And this is Grandma Aggie, and that's Mom."

Gwen came into the kitchen, looking frazzled.

She had a floppy straw hat on her head, a duffel bag in her hand, and a camera hanging from her neck.

"Okay, I've got my passport, my ticket, my sunscreen, my bathing suit . . . Ooh! I forgot my bathing suit—" Gwen started to turn, then stopped, noticing the six-foot scarecrow in her kitchen. "Hi, I'm Gwen. It's so nice to meet you. Sorry things are a bit hectic around here."

"No worries, Mrs. Piper. I'm just goin' with the flow." He looked sheepishly at Marnie, to see if she'd noticed how polite and laid-back he was.

"Great. 'Go with the flow,'" repeated Gwen, moving her hand in a wave motion in front of her. "Excuse me, I've got to get my bathing suit." She hurried out of the kitchen.

Marnie started setting the table for lunch. "So, Fred, how are you liking things over at the lab? Dylan thinks he's died and gone to heaven, watching beakers bubble all summer."

"Um, it's great. Yeah. We're working on lots of important stuff," said Fred, standing up taller.

"You make fun now . . ." Dylan said, plopping down at his usual place at the table, "but one day I'll be recognized as a hero. We're discovering the fountain of youth!"

"The fountain of youth?" asked Marnie, skeptically raising an eyebrow, as she set a napkin in front of her brother. "Well, the whole thing kind of gives me the creeps. There are some things you just shouldn't mess with."

"I agree," said Aggie, an anxious look on her face as she ladled chili into bowls. "There's something about that La Biel I've never trusted."

She accidentally spilled a glob of chili on the table. "Oops!" she said, waving a hand over it as it magically disappeared.

"Gwen," she called, "lunch is ready! Take a seat wherever you'd like, Fred," Aggie said warmly.

Fred sat next to Marnie.

After lunch, as the pots scrubbed themselves, the family—and Fred—gathered outside to help Gwen load her luggage into the cab.

"I'll help you with that," Fred said, trying to take a suitcase from Marnie's hands.

"It's okay. I've got it," she objected.

As they both pulled, the suitcase fell open, spilling shorts and T-shirts all over the lawn. Marnie and Fred both bent down to pick up the spilled clothes, knocking heads in the process.

"It's all right," Gwen laughed. "I've got it."

With a snap, the clothes folded and packed themselves back into the suitcase. It clicked shut and floated into the backseat.

"Okay," she sighed. "This is it!"

Marnie went to her mother's open arms for a good-bye hug.

"I don't know about this. I've never left you all for this long before!" Gwen said, teary eyed, over Marnie's shoulder.

"It'll be okay, my dear," Aggie assured her. She patted her daughter on the back.

"You realize you're in charge now?" asked Gwen, looking sternly at her mother.

"Of course! Of course!" Aggie fluttered her hands as if this were a small matter.

"And you, my dear," Gwen said, turning back to Marnie, "are to look after Sophie." Marnie nodded. "Fred," she added, "you look after Dylan."

"You got it, Mrs. P.," Fred said, grinning.

"Hey!" Dylan protested.

Gwen slid into the cab's backseat. "To Hawaii," she instructed the cab driver, who turned his bony head. It was Benny the skeleton from Halloweentown! "Benny, what are you doing in the mortal world?" she asked, surprised.

"Special delivery." His jaw bone moved up and down as he chuckled.

Benny tipped his hat to Aggie and the kids and flew off with Gwen to the airport.

CHAPTER THREE

So far, Sophie was loving summer school. What wasn't to love? She got to hang out with Stephanie and Sylvie and do cool magic all day. But her favorite class, without a doubt, was Broom Driver's Ed.

Covering safety tips and traffic laws had been a little boring, but this week they were actually on brooms. Of course, they still had to ride with an instructor, but it was thrilling nonetheless. Sophie had never seen Halloweentown from that vantage point before. Perched on her broomstick, flying high above the ground with the wind in her hair, she could pick out the orange blob of the Great Pumpkin, Town Hall, even Grandma Aggie's house.

Today the focus was on "defensive flying." Young witches were ten times more likely to have broom accidents. "Assume the worst," their instructor had told them, "and act accordingly."

Unfortunately, Sophie hadn't assumed the worst when class had first begun, and it had happened. She'd been hoping to be assigned Stephanie or Sylvie as a flying partner. Instead, she'd gotten Stan. Stan was a red-haired, freckle-faced, buck-toothed warlock who smelled vaguely of mushrooms and had a tendency to stare at her.

Sophie now stood with Sylvie and Stephanie in the middle of the Witch U. quad, waiting for class to begin. Some of the students were late. Their instructor Mr. Midgley, a short warlock with a huge nose, was pacing with his clipboard and mumbling to himself about punctuality.

The girls were giggling about the latest

episode of their favorite TV show in which the main character, a troll named Sabrina, lost a bet with her best friend and had to shave her bright pink hair into a Mohawk. As their laughter died down, Sophie suddenly got quiet.

Stephanie noticed and reached out to touch her friend's arm. "What's wrong, Soph?" she asked.

"I don't know," Sophie said. She wrinkled her forehead. "You know how sometimes I get that weird feeling that someone's coming? Someone bad, usually?"

"Yeah . . ." the other two girls said in unison.

"Well," Sophie shivered slightly, "I have that feeling now."

"Maybe it's just nerves about our potions test coming up?" Sylvie suggested.

"No." Sophie shook her head, trying to shake off the feeling. "It's not nerves. Forget it. It's probably just—"

Sophie was interrupted by Stan, who appeared at her side, edging his way into the girls' circle.

He was out of breath from running to class. He leaned over and put his hands on his knees.

"Sorry I'm late, Sophie," he panted. "Had some business to attend to."

"Maybe *there's* the reason for your feeling," Stephanie whispered under her breath. Sylvie giggled.

Sophie, who was trying to hold back her own laughter, shot Stephanie a look, but Stan hadn't heard. He was looking intently at Sophie.

"I'll make it up to you," he said.

"Really, Stan," Sophie insisted, "there's no need."

Stan wasn't the only one running late. Professor Periwinkle was already in the classroom when Aggie finally arrived. Her alligator handbag crawled dutifully behind her.

Both of the older witches were excited. This summer's students had done exceptionally well in their class so far, despite being only Level One witches and warlocks. But that had been the easy stuff: slowing down and fast-forwarding time. *Now* came the hard part: stopping time. The flow of time, after all, was not an easy thing to control, even if just for a few seconds or minutes. Only the best witches ever truly got the hang of it.

Professor Periwinkle was looking over her notes, her eyeglasses perched on the tip of her button nose. "Hello, Aggie," she sang pleasantly. "Perhaps we need to give *you* a course in time management," she teased, looking at the clock.

"Oh, Persimmon, I'm sorry for the delay. I was preparing my morning tea when Gwen appeared from Hawaii in my pot of water. She's been gone just a few days, but you'd think she'd been gone for an age! She keeps checking in to see how the kids are. She doesn't have much confidence in her old mother, I'm afraid." Aggie shook her head sadly.

"They never do, my dear. They never do," clucked Persimmon Periwinkle. "My Amber's the same way."

Just then the students started to file into the classroom: a dozen teenaged witches and warlocks with backpacks slung haphazardly over their shoulders. Professor Periwinkle had to remind some of them to leave their starter brooms outside.

"Well," said Aggie, clasping her hands together in front of the class. "Today the real fun begins!"

"Who here has ever been in a situation where you wished you could stop time?" asked Professor Periwinkle. Every student raised a hand. "As I thought. Then watch very carefully, because time-freezing is difficult."

"Shall we start them with the invocation?" asked Aggie brightly.

"No, let us begin with the spell," insisted Professor Periwinkle.

"I always start with the invocation," Aggie whispered.

"And I always start with the spell," Professor Periwinkle whispered back. She was adamant.

The two witches turned so the class couldn't hear. The students gave each other questioning looks behind their teachers' backs while they were whispering.

"Well, let's try it!" said Aggie finally.

Professor Periwinkle nodded and they turned. Closing her eyes, she said, "Erwind temperatum temporalis."

Suddenly the world lurched into reverse. The students started to file out the door backwards, and Aggie fed her wand to her alligator hand-bag.

"Oh dear!" exclaimed Persimmon. She'd said the wrong spell. She quickly recited it backward: "Silaropmet mutarepmet dniwre."

The students returned to their seats, and the alligator bag spit out Aggie's wand.

"Well," Aggie said again. "Today the real fun begins! Shall we start with the invocation?"

Talk about déjà vu!

"Yes, why don't we try that," Professor Periwinkle agreed.

This time Aggie closed her eyes, chanting the invocation first and then the spell.

But once again, the class rose from their seats, shuffling backward from the classroom. Professor Periwinkle glanced at the clock, then lowered her head to her notes. Reverse time again!

"Oops!" cried Aggie. "Silaropmet mutarepmet dniwre," she said quickly.

"I think we might have the wrong spell, Persimmon," Aggie whispered, once everyone had returned to the present.

"Let me check my notes," replied Periwinkle. She bowed her strawberry blond head over her notebook. "Ah," she said, pointing to a page. "Yes, I see. You begin."

Once more Aggie closed her eyes and started with the invocation: "Pater Tiempo, grant us this spell, that we may use your power well. Your never-ending nature we know and ask your help to change the flow . . ."

"*Arrestum* temperatum temporalis," Professor Periwinkle continued.

Time froze. The students sat, pens poised above paper. One girl with her mouth hanging open prepared to chomp down on her gum. A young witch named Susan was passing a note to her friend Lenore.

Professor Periwinkle and Aggie smiled at each other. "Well done," said Periwinkle.

"Not bad yourself," winked Aggie. She took the note from Susan's hand. "Shall we?"

Both witches snapped their fingers and time resumed. Susan looked around her desk, thinking she'd dropped her note.

"Now pay attention," Periwinkle and Aggie said in unison, tapping their wands on the desk.

Sophie opened the door to her dorm room. The overwhelming smell of vegetation greeted her. She sneezed.

"What are these?" asked a confused Stephanie.

Sophie groaned. "Weeds."

"Why?" Sylvie asked, stepping into the room. It was overflowing with ragweed, milkweed, and dandelions. There was a thin coat of yellow pollen covering every surface of the room.

"I'll give you one guess," answered an annoyed Sophie.

"Stan," Stephanie and Sylvie said at once.

"Yep. ACHOOO! This is the second time he's done this. I think he's trying to fill my room with flowers. AH-AH-ACHOOO! Only he hasn't quite mastered the spell yet."

Sophie stepped over thorns and itchy green leaves. She turned in a circle, surveying the mess, and sneezed again.

"Is he *still* bugging you?" Sylvie asked.

"You could say that," Sophie grumbled, as a centipede crawled from a clump of thistle onto her shoe. She shook the bug off.

Since being teamed up with Sophie in Broom Driver's Ed, Stan had looked her up online and instantly began e-mailing her. Lately, he'd gotten more adventurous in his amorous activities, making love notes appear on the steamed mirror in Sophie's bathroom and filling her room with what she guessed were *supposed* to be roses. She could only assume this most recent gesture was to make up for being late the other day.

There was a knock at Sophie's door. It was Marnie and Ethan—together as always, thought Sophie.

"Hey, Soph. Just wanted to check in," Marnie said, looking around at the plant life strewn over Sophie's desk, bed, and floor. "What's all this?"

"Stan," Sophie answered, her hands on her hips. "He . . . he . . . he . . . ACHOO," she sneezed. "He won't leave me alone."

"Stan?" asked Ethan. Stan was in his dorm. In fact, it was Stan who had needed help moving his trunk the first day. "Aw, he's a nice guy. He's just a little . . ."

"Dorky?" guessed Stephanie.

"Weird?" asked Sylvie.

"Annoying!" exclaimed Sophie.

"Different," Ethan finished. "But you should give him a chance, Sophie. It seems," he said, looking around at the weeds, "he really likes you."

Ethan was cute and a great guy. Sophie could see why Marnie liked him so much—even loved him, she suspected—but he just didn't get it. She looked at him sideways now. "I don't think so."

Ethan shrugged. "I tried, Pumpkin," he said, putting his arm around Marnie's shoulders.

"Marnie, can you do something about this?" Sophie asked, desperately gesturing at the weeds.

Marnie pulled her wand from her sleeve, and with a few blasts around the room, the weeds were gone. "Other than Stan, how are classes going?" she asked when she had finished.

"Fine," Sophie assured her. "I learned some cool stuff in clairvoyance class. But Mom won't stop calling."

"I know." Marnie rolled her eyes. "I tell her to relax, but . . ."

"She won't," sighed Sophie.

Marnie wrapped her arm around Ethan's waist. "Well, we're off," she said. "I told Ethan I'd go to the batball game with him."

"She can almost tell which team is which," he laughed.

"How exciting for her," said Sophie sarcastically. Marnie shot her a warning glance. "Have fun," Sophie said, shutting the door behind them.

As she did, Sophie's face lit up. She had an idea. "I bet I can foresee the score of the batball game! We worked on numbers in clairvoyance yesterday."

"How much?" challenged Sylvie.

Sophie thought for a second. "My hair!"

"Deal," said a delighted Sylvie, sticking out her hand to shake on it.

"See, I knew you were going to say that," grinned Sophie.

CHAPTER
FOUR

Professor Lucius La Biel was very agitated. He was so close! But there were still a few ingredients to his youth serum that evaded him. He paced around the lab, talking to himself as his team of researchers and assistants exchanged worried glances. Suddenly he stopped, tapping his head beneath his wild, gray hair.

"What do babies do?" he asked, looking at one of the researchers.

"Sleep?" responded the surprised doctor.

"Yes, but no!" La Biel shouted, pointing at another doctor.

"Eat?"

"No! You!" La Biel pointed at Fred.

"Um, my baby sister poops a lot."

"No! Dylan?"

"Cry?" asked a stunned Dylan.

La Biel was quiet for a second, thinking. His eyes were crazy behind his thick, black-framed glasses. "You've got something there, Dylan, my boy," he said.

La Biel looked at the blackboard, and a piece of chalk floated into the air. It began to scrawl a complicated formula on the chalkboard.

"Yes!" he shouted a moment later when the formula was complete. "Yes," he repeated in a strange voice, looking intently at Dylan. Then, without another word, La Biel left the lab and went to his office, the door slamming behind him.

Everyone looked at Dylan, who shrugged. Suddenly, another agitated scientist entered the lab: Dr. Rosenblumen. His face was red, and he furiously wiped at the shoulder of his white lab coat with a handkerchief.

"Ahh! Zee birds!" he huffed. "Zey are always vaiting for me. Just coo, coo, cooing on zee roof. Zen zey drop zese 'presents' on me." He grimaced, pointing at the goopy brown spot on his white coat.

A flock of pigeons had taken to perching on the roof, right above the entrance to the research center. They liked to hit people as they came in and out of the building. Dylan himself had narrowly missed a nice, drippy mess on his own head that morning.

Rosenblumen put down his briefcase, pulling out a fresh lab coat and tossing the soiled one aside. "Fred," he said, "I need you to go to zee roof and get rid of zem."

"How do I do that, Dr. Rosenblumen?"

"I don't know! You are zee scarecrow!" he exclaimed impatiently. "Just scare zem avay."

Fred started to protest, then realized it

was useless. He headed for the stairs as the rest of the team went back to their more exciting jobs.

The sun was bright on the building's rooftop, and Fred had to squint his eyes to see. About twenty pigeons swiveled their heads to watch Fred's tall, lanky figure coming toward them. They weren't scared, however, and quickly turned back to watch the entrance below for more potential victims.

"Dudes, sorry to disturb you, but I'm gonna have to ask you to leave," Fred told the birds.

They didn't move. He tried shooing them with his hands, but they stayed put.

"Okay. You're a scarecrow," Fred said aloud to himself. "Be scary. Boo!" he shouted. No response. The pigeons practically yawned.

Finally, fed up, Fred began to wildly flail his long arms and legs. He lunged at the birds like a madman. They scattered, some flying away but most relocating to a rusty water tower on the corner of the roof. As Fred once again moved toward the birds, he heard the door to the roof creak open. Peeking around the edge of the water tank, Fred saw it was La Biel.

The professor glanced nervously around the roof. Unable to see Fred behind the large water tank, La Biel assumed he was alone. Pulling out his cellular witch's glass, he raised it into the air as if he were looking for better reception. Finding a suitable spot, he flipped open the tiny, palm-sized mirror and placed a call.

"It's me," he said. The tone of his voice was secretive, not like the voice he used in the lab. "I told you not to call me at work. . . . No, it's fine now. I'm on the roof." He sounded irritated.

"Don't get your witch's britches in a twist!" he told the person on the other end of the line. "Everything's going according to plan. Believe me when I tell you, Dylan doesn't suspect a thing. He'd give me anything I asked for—in the name of science, of course." La Biel let out a high-pitched cackle.

All of a sudden, Fred felt very uncomfortable.

He stood stock-still hoping La Biel wouldn't discover him behind the tank. He didn't know what the professor was talking about, but it didn't sound good.

Luckily, La Biel snapped his cellular glass shut and quickly exited the roof through the creaky, metal door.

Fred peered around the tank and waited till he was sure La Biel had gone before coming out into the open. In his puzzled daze, he tripped on a loose board, sending the pigeons flying every which way. Fred composed himself. He had to tell Dylan what he'd overheard—now!

Sophie hurried up the steps and through the doors of the research center, where her potions class met in one of the science labs. They had a test today. Sophie, who'd stayed up late watching movies with Sylvie and Stephanie, hadn't exactly studied as much as she should have. Technically, though, she still had two more minutes to cram.

With her head bent over her notes as she

dashed down the hall, Sophie barely saw the man in the white lab coat before she ran smack into him. Her notebook went flying and pieces of paper fluttered to the floor around her.

"Oh, I'm sorry!" Sophie exclaimed. She looked up to find the man she'd practically bowled over was none other than Professor Lucius La Biel. She'd seen his picture in *The Halloweentown Herald* just a few days before in an article about his youth serum.

"I'm sorry, Miss Piper," said La Biel. "I should have watched where I was going."

The professor gathered her notebook and papers with a quick, magic flick of the hand. He handed them back to Sophie.

Something about La Biel made Sophie feel very uneasy. She chalked it up to the white coat. Sophie had never liked going to the doctor as a kid. But this man wasn't a *doctor* doctor; he was a scientist.

"You have a test today, Miss Piper?" he asked, smiling strangely.

It dawned on Sophie that La Biel was using her

name. How did he know who she was? She'd never met him! And her picture certainly wasn't in the paper! Her heart leaped into her throat.

"Yeah," she answered carefully. "I better get going," she said, starting to slide around him.

But La Biel sidestepped, blocking her way. "You know, I have a very quiet, safe place where you can do all the studying you want. You'll even have a study buddy!"

The professor's voice was frightening Sophie now. She clutched her notebook to her and stared at him coldly. "I really don't think—"

Again, he stepped in front of her as she tried to pass him.

"Don't worry," he said, holding up his witch's glass. "We'll know how to find you when we need you."

"Slow down, Fred, and tell me again what you think you heard," Dylan said.

They were sitting in the skating park, but Fred was still whispering as if La Biel might somehow

42

overhear them. "He said you would give him *whatever* he wanted. He's using you, man," Fred said impatiently.

Dylan balked at that idea. "Using me? For what? Maybe he just values my assistance," he said, his pride obviously hurt by the notion that La Biel's intentions would be anything less than sterling.

"He's definitely planning something, dude." Strands of golden, strawlike hair stuck out from under Fred's baseball cap and they trembled as he shook his head. "It gives me the willies, personally."

"Are you jealous, Fred?" Dylan asked, staring angrily at his friend. "Because La Biel is giving me more responsibility? Is that what this, this . . . slander . . . is all about?" He was getting worked up, and his voice was rising.

Fred stared at him, stung by the accusation. "No, man! I promise. I heard it with my own two ears, on the roof."

"Yeah, well, you have straw in your ears,"

Dylan snapped. He rose from the bench they were sitting on. "I think I've had enough skateboarding for today," he said. "See you tomorrow."

Fred watched helplessly as Dylan stalked away.

As he walked back into the research center to pick up his magicbiology book, Dylan fumed.

How dare Fred make such accusations? He was just jealous because La Biel saw potential in Dylan. Dylan could be a *real* scientist one day. All Fred was really good for was cleaning beakers and shooing away birds!

In his frustration, Dylan kicked open the door to the lab. He was alarmed to find La Biel standing on the other side. The professor was holding a test tube over an open flame as the liquid inside snapped and crackled.

"Hello, Dylan," the professor greeted him warmly. "Did you forget something?"

"Hi, Professor La Biel. Sorry about the door. I just wanted to get my book."

"Quite all right, my boy," replied La Biel.

"Actually, Dylan, there's something I've been meaning to tell you."

"Yes?" asked Dylan, hoping for some piece of praise or a hint as to how the experiments were coming along.

Instead, La Biel looked up from the flame and directly at Dylan. "Oblivio memori," he intoned.

Dylan blinked.

"Did you forget something, Dylan?" La Biel asked again.

Dylan looked around the lab with a puzzled expression on his face. "I thought so, but I can't remember what it was now!" He gave out a little laugh and shook his head at his own forgetfulness.

"Your book?" La Biel asked, nodding at the magicbiology book on the counter.

"That was it!" Dylan grabbed it. "Thanks, Professor La Biel. See you tomorrow," he said, turning to go.

"Until then, Dylan."

CHAPTER
FIVE

"**I** know exactly what La Biel's after," said Marnie.

Fred had appeared at her door just minutes before. It was important, he'd said—something about Dylan. Hearing Marnie say this now, Fred was glad he'd come to her.

"The Gift," Marnie continued.

"What's that?" Fred asked. He sat at Marnie's desk, looking at her framed family picture-videos. She was pacing the room, deep in thought.

"An amulet. It's a Cromwell family heirloom. It

was my grandmother's, and she passed it on to me." Fred gave her an odd look. "I'm still a Cromwell witch even if my last name is Piper. *Anyway*, it's extremely powerful and gives whoever wears it ultimate power over hearts and minds. Basically," she said, stopping and staring intently at Fred, "the witch—or warlock—who wears it, rules Halloweentown."

Fred's eyes grew as big as saucers.

"Last year, after Dr. Goodwin and the Dominion tried to get control of it, I secretly gave it to Dylan for safekeeping. La Biel must have figured it out somehow."

"Whoa," Fred murmured in awe. He hadn't known what he'd overheard was *that* big of a deal!

"We have to get it from Dylan immediately," said Marnie, already heading toward the door.

Fred stood and hastily followed Marnie.

"What do you mean, you don't remember where you put it?" asked an increasingly annoyed Marnie.

She and Fred had found Dylan in his room, speed reading a magicbiology textbook. Unfortunately, he wasn't proving to be much of a help in locating the Gift.

"I know I had it at some point," said Dylan, as if in a fog, "but I just can't seem to recall where I hid it."

He looked around his room, squinting as if he were trying to summon an old memory. Marnie took him by the shoulders and looked him in the eye.

"Pull yourself together, Dylan. I'm not joking around. Fred is serious. La Biel wants the Gift. You have to tell me where it is."

"I just can't remember. . . ." His voice faded.

Marnie threw up her hands and went to the window, gazing out at the courtyard in silence. Fred joined her.

Finally, she looked at Fred. "This just isn't like Dylan. Trust me, he doesn't forget *anything*—especially if he can use it against me later," she said under her breath. "La Biel must have cast a spell of forgetting on him. He must have known we were coming."

Fred nodded his head solemnly. "So what do we do? Can we make him, like, *un*forget?"

"Well," answered Marnie, her hands on her hips, "it's a powerful spell, but I think I can reverse it. Grandma Aggie taught me. I just need the name of the person who cast it."

She closed her eyes for a second, conjuring up the words for the remembering spell, then turned to Dylan. She raised her hands in front of her, palms out.

"Restoratum memori edwyn por La Biel!" she chanted.

A bluish-purple light glowed around Marnie's hands. Dylan blinked behind his glasses.

"Do you remember where the Gift is now?" Marnie asked. She and Fred looked hopefully at Dylan.

"What gift?" Dylan said, looking back and forth between his sister and his friend. "Is it someone's birthday?" he added excitedly.

"Shoot! Let me try again," Marnie said. Once more, she put her hands out toward Dylan. "Restoratum memori edwyn por La Biel!"

They looked at Dylan. Nothing.

"Sorry to be rude, guys, but I really should get back to studying," said Dylan, opening the door to signal to his guests that it was time to leave.

"But . . ." started Fred. If La Biel had designs on the Gift, they needed to get it before he did!

Marnie took his hand and led him out of the room. "It's okay, Fred," she assured him. "We won't get anywhere with Dylan like this. Maybe I have the spell wrong. I have a spell book in my room. So let's let the bookworm get back to his studying and we can double-check."

"So, the spell book should be somewhere in that bookcase," Marnie said a short while later, as she and Fred entered her room. She pointed to shelves that lined almost an entire wall of her room. They reached nearly fifteen feet from floor to ceiling.

Fred's head bent back as he surveyed the search area. There must have been a thousand books on those shelves! The bookcase was more than twice his height!

"Somewhere in there?" he asked again, hoping maybe he'd misheard the first time.

"Yep," Marnie confirmed. She also peered up at the daunting sight.

"Well," Fred gulped, "do you have a ladder?"

Fred wasn't fond of heights. He had fallen once as a kid, when he chased a woodpecker out onto an unsteady tree limb. He had broken his arm so badly, he'd needed an arm transplant. But he didn't want to look like a scaredy-cat in front of Marnie now!

"I can do even better than a ladder." Marnie winked at him.

Suddenly, Fred felt weightless. He looked down to find himself floating inches off the floor.

"Whoa," he said. "This is awesome."

Marnie smiled, and Fred rose higher, almost to the top of the bookshelf. He did a somersault in

51

the air, accidentally knocking a book off the shelf.

"Whoops!" he exclaimed.

Marnie quickly pointed at the falling book. It slowed, finally fluttering to a stop in her hands.

"Is that the spell book?" Fred asked, looking down at Marnie from above.

"Nope," Marnie replied, unaware of his thoughts. "It's my invocation textbook. Keep looking."

Fred went left to right, down the rows of books, reading the titles from the book spines.

"*The Odyssey?*"

"No," Marnie answered from below.

"*The History of Halloweentown?*"

"Nope."

"*Moby Dick?*"

"Definitely not."

"*The Terminology of Trances?*"

"Now *that* was a real fun class," Marnie said sarcastically, shaking her head.

Fred decided to take a different tactic. "Do you remember what color it was?" he asked, floating in midair.

Marnie thought for a second. "Red," she said. "No, no. Brown."

"Brown?" Fred asked.

"Brown," Marnie repeated. "Or, maybe, it was red. . . ."

"Okay, well, it's either red or brown," said Fred. "That narrows it down to about—" He examined the bookshelf. "—five hundred books."

Marnie sighed. She leaned her shoulder against the bookshelf.

"How are we ever going to . . ." she stopped short. In front of her nose was a navy book. In gold cursive, its spine read simply, *Spells*.

"Or maybe it was blue." She smiled up at Fred as she pulled out the book.

Marnie blew on the book's cover and coughed at the cloud of dust it produced.

"It's been a while since I needed this. I guess that's a good thing!" she said.

She returned Fred to the floor. He stood beside her, fascinated by the glowing pages as Marnie flipped through the book. Standing so close to her, it occurred to Fred that Marnie didn't just look good, she also smelled good. He had the urge to ask her out.

"Um, Marnie . . ." he started.

"Yeah, Fred?" she asked distractedly.

"Would you wanna . . . I mean, would you like to—"

"Aha!" she shouted, cutting him off. She opened the book wide to a page in the center. "Here it is: 'The Spell of Remembering.'"

Marnie and Fred sat on the stone bench outside her dorm as students passed by on their way to class. Fred's large head was in his hands. Marnie was slumped down.

"I just don't get it!" she exclaimed, shaking her head. "I had the spell right *and* La Biel's name. It should have worked."

They sat in frustrated silence.

Marnie remembered something: "Fred, didn't you start to ask me a question in my room?"

"Oh. Yeah. Um, actually, I was wondering—"

Marnie's face suddenly brightened. She sat up. "Unless La Biel's not the professor's real name!" she exclaimed.

Fred's eyes widened. "That would explain it," he agreed.

Looking up, Marnie's face grew brighter. Ethan was crossing the courtyard toward them.

"Hey. I've been looking for you everywhere," Ethan said to Marnie as he approached the bench. He was slightly out of breath. He glanced at Fred, then back to Marnie. "It's Sophie."

"What's up?" Marnie asked, her expression instantly growing serious.

"Stan told me she didn't show up for Broom Flyer's Ed today."

"That's her favorite class," said Marnie.

"I know."

Marnie furrowed her eyebrows.

Ethan glanced again at Fred. "Hi, I'm Ethan," he said, reaching out to shake the skater's twiggy hand.

"Fred."

"Sorry," said a distracted Marnie. "This is

Dylan's friend from the lab. *That's* a whole nother story," she said, sighing heavily.

"What happened?" asked Ethan.

"We don't have time to explain," Marnie replied brusquely. "Ethan, why don't you ask around the dorms about Sophie? Start with Sylvie and Stephanie. I have a feeling my darling sister and her friends might have just opted for a day of shopping at Halloweentown Mall instead of class. Fred, you and I need to go see my grandmother."

Ethan tried to hide his dismay. Who was this guy hanging around Marnie? How come Ethan hadn't met him before today? Before his suspicion could even register, Marnie and Fred were up and on their way to the building where Aggie was teaching.

"Thanks," Marnie called to Ethan over her shoulder.

"Sure," he mumbled.

CHAPTER
SIX

"Hello, dears!" Aggie greeted Marnie and Fred warmly.

She pointed her wand at the chalkboard. An eraser quickly scrolled down and then up, as if blinking, and revealed a blank slate.

"What lucky occasion brings you to my classroom?"

"Grandma, we have a problem," confided Marnie. She took a seat in one of the student desks. "You might want to sit down, too."

Aggie snapped her fingers, and a stool appeared next to her. Fred eagerly relayed the conversation he'd overheard on the roof, and Marnie explained how they'd deduced that La Biel—or whatever his name was—was looking to get his hands on the Gift.

"You know, I've always had a feeling about that warlock. He reminds me of someone, but I can't put my finger on . . ." Aggie faded off, wrinkling her brow as if she were trying hard to remember something.

"*And* Sophie missed her favorite class today. We don't know where she is," Marnie added.

Aggie pursed her lips. "Yes, this is bad," she said. The look on her face confirmed it.

Suddenly, a ringing sound came from Aggie's bag. She reached in and rummaged around for her cellular witch's glass. "I can't ever find this darn thing . . ." she grumbled as she reached her entire arm, up to the shoulder, into the bag.

Finally, she pulled out the witch's glass and looked at the caller ID. "It's your mother," she said anxiously. "Should we tell her?"

Marnie looked torn. The phone continued to ring. Aggie picked up, and Gwen appeared in the glass. She was sitting on a beach, the blue surf lapping at white sand behind her. A floppy straw hat shielded her eyes, and a bright pink lei hung around her neck. She held a frozen juice drink topped with a pineapple slice.

"Hello, dear!" Aggie said, a little too excitedly. "How is Hawaii?"

"Hi, Mother. Oh, it's wonderful!" Gwen said, smiling.

Marnie waved her hands wildly as her grandmother and mother chatted, signaling to Aggie not to say a word about Dylan or Sophie. Her mother was finally getting some well-deserved rest and relaxation time. There was nothing she could do from Hawaii, anyway. Marnie would get the situation under control.

Aggie looked anxiously at Marnie, then back at Gwen in the witch's glass.

Gwen stopped talking about her tennis lessons

with the resort pro and asked suspiciously, "Who are you looking at?"

"No one!" said Aggie, nervously smoothing her hair.

"Mother, is something going on?"

Marnie, out of sight of the witch's glass, shook her head and mouthed the word "no."

"No, of course not," insisted Aggie casually. "Professor Periwinkle is here. We have to prepare for class. Glad you're having fun, dear. Do call again soon!"

"Mother . . ." Gwen's voice called, as Aggie quickly snapped the witch's glass shut.

As soon as Aggie's was closed, Marnie's cell glass started ringing to the tune of "Monster Mash." Fred chuckled.

"Aneesa programmed it," said Marnie. "It's probably Mom."

She looked down at the caller ID. "No, it's Ethan. . . . Hello," she said as Ethan appeared in the mirror's surface.

"Hey. No sign of Sophie. Sylvie and Stephanie

said they haven't seen her since she headed to the science lab for Perfectly Potent Potions class this morning."

"The science lab?" repeated Marnie, shooting a concerned look at Aggie and Fred. "Hmmm. Thanks, Ethan. I'll call you later." She hung up. "Something's wrong. I can see why La Biel wants the Gift, but what would Sophie have to do with all of this?"

"I'm not sure," said Aggie, "but I do know nine times out of ten, a missing witch can be found in a witch's glass."

"What about the tenth time?" asked Fred. Aggie and Marnie gave him a warning look that said they didn't want to discuss it. He gulped.

"We'll have to split up," said Marnie, taking charge. "Grandma, you go looking for Sophie. Fred and I will unlock the secret of La Biel. Any suggestions?"

"Yes, actually," said Aggie. She tapped a finger thoughtfully on her mouth. "There is one."

Marnie and Fred listened intently.

"Beyond the city, almost to the limits of Halloweentown, there's a forest. In that forest, lives an old witch named Rumora. She used to be Halloweentown's local gossip queen." At this, Aggie raised a disapproving eyebrow. "If anyone knows something about Lucius La Biel, it's her."

"How do we get there?" asked Fred.

"Well, over the river and through the woods, of course," said Aggie. "Just follow the compass."

Aggie snapped her fingers, and in the scarecrow's hand appeared a small compass. Only instead of pointing North, it pointed to a picture of a small cottage.

"Great," said Marnie, not hesitating. "Let's go."

"There's only one thing," Aggie called after them as they headed out the door. "She's a little crotchety."

A while later, Fred and Marnie stood in a wide clearing in the forest. Fred was staring down at the compass.

"I knew I should have been an Eagle Scout," he said to Marnie. She peered through the dim light that filtered down between the trees. "But my dad said it was 'for the birds.'"

They were lost. Terribly lost. They had ridden Marnie's broom to the edge of the forest but had to abandon it there. The tall trees were too dense. Marnie gazed up at them now, looking for the sun to give her a clue as to which direction she and Fred were headed. The forest was spooky, and it was starting to get chilly. Marnie would be happy to find Rumora and get out of there.

"Let me see," she said, reaching out for the compass. She aligned the arrow, hoping it would point to the cottage, but it pointed to where they'd just come from! It didn't make sense!

"Are you looking for someone?" asked a voice.

"Of course, I am. So are you!" said Marnie, thinking it was Fred's voice she'd heard.

"I didn't say that," said Fred.

"Then who did?" Marnie asked, glancing around the clearing.

"I did," said the voice again.

Fred and Marnie spun around. No one was there.

"Who . . . who are you?" asked Fred, unable to conceal the fear in his voice.

"I'm me. . . ."

Fred and Marnie looked toward the sound of the voice. For the first time, they noticed a tree unlike the rest. Rather than branches that grew up to the sky, the long, leafy branches of this tree arched over like whips. What looked like knobs and folds in the bark formed a face. A hole in the trunk was a mouth that moved as the tree talked.

"Willow," it said. "That's my name. Are you here to visit me?"

Marnie approached the tree. "No, we're looking for Rumora, a witch who lives in a cottage near here. Do you know where we might find her?"

"You mean you're not here to see me?" the tree asked, its mouth drooping into a frown.

"No, we're here to find Rumora," repeated Marnie.

Suddenly the tree erupted in sobs. Its long, thin branches shook under the weight of its weeping. "No one ever comes to see me!" it wailed.

"Oh, it's okay," said Marnie, caressing the trunk. "We'll come back and see you. We just need to find Rumora first. Can you tell us which way to go."

Willow whimpered. "You promise? You'll come back and see me?"

"Of course," said Fred, pulling a bandana out of his pocket and using it to blot the sappy tears from the tree's trunk.

"Okay," sniffled Willow, who raised a single branch and pointed in the direction of Rumora's cottage. "It's just half a mile past the bridge. Watch out for Sparky."

"Thanks!" Marnie said, patting the trunk.

"Who's Sparky?" wondered Fred, as they started in the direction Willow had pointed.

Marnie shrugged. "Beats me. But let's make like a tree and leave!"

* * *

Before long, as Willow had said, Marnie and Fred came to a small footbridge. But Fred hadn't taken his first step onto the bridge before a small troll appeared out of nowhere, blocking the way. Fred jumped back.

"'Ello!" said the troll, who came barely to Fred's waist. "Sparky here. I'm afraid you are not going anywhere until you answer three riddles!" he said, spitting in excitement.

Fred looked back at Marnie. "It's okay," she said. "I'm good at riddles. Shoot!" she said to the troll.

Sparky opened his mouth but stopped. He furrowed his fuzzy, caterpillarlike eyebrows and wrinkled his warty nose.

"Now 'old on a second. I know this . . ." he said, wagging a stumpy finger at Marnie and Fred. He turned his back to them and mumbled to himself, scratching his bald head. "What do you get when you cross a . . . No, that's not it. How many . . . No, that isn't it either. . . ."

"Excuse me, Mr. Sparky . . ." Marnie tried.

"Just gimme a minute!" the troll shouted. "We

don't get many visitors roun' here, but . . . Ah! Got it. You have five . . . no, three . . . *Bah!*" He threw his hairy arms into the air.

"Fine. It's your lucky day, I s'pose," he grumbled and stepped out of the way.

Fred and Marnie silently walked past him and over the bridge.

"Thanks, man," said Fred when they were on the other side. Sparky only grumbled.

"There it is!" Marnie finally called, rushing through the trees toward a small cottage with smoke rising from the chimney. She and Fred ran to the door.

Marnie knocked. There were rumblings from inside, the sound of pots banging, and of a pig snorting. Suddenly, the door creaked open. An old, hunched-over woman stood behind it. Her eyes were milky and blue. She was blind.

"Hi. I'm sorry to bother you. I'm Marnie and this is Fred." Fred was examining the house upclose. Marnie poked him in the ribs.

The old witch reached out and touched Marnie's face, running her withered hands over the girl's features.

"Are you Rumora?" Marnie asked, when she was done. The woman nodded but said nothing.

"Your house is made of gingerbread!" blurted Fred.

The old woman winced but opened the door, beckoning them to come inside. Marnie shot him a glance and silently shushed him with a finger to her lips.

The cottage was cramped and dark, the only light coming from several dripping candles and a potbellied stove that glowed in the corner. Something fragrant simmered in a large cauldron in the center of the room. In a dark corner, a large pig lay on a burlap sack, watching them.

The old witch motioned for Fred and Marnie to sit on two rickety chairs around the cauldron. She pulled up a third.

"We need your help," said Marnie, figuring she ought to get straight to the point. "We need you to tell us about Lucius La Biel."

Rumora drew in a quick breath. "I don't talk about other people," she hissed.

"It's very important," insisted Fred. "The fate of Halloweentown could depend on it!"

Rumora seemed unimpressed. "I said, 'I don't talk about other people.'" Her unseeing eyes swiveled in their sockets.

Marnie shifted uncomfortably in her seat and began to protest, but Rumora stopped her short. "I smell a mortal," she said, leaning toward Marnie. The witch herself smelled like garlic.

"I—I'm half-mortal," Marnie said, gulping. This old witch was making her uncomfortable.

"Do you know Hansel and Gretel?" Rumora asked, cocking her head suspiciously.

"No," Marnie answered, shaking her head. "They're just characters in a fairy tale."

"A fairy tale?" repeated the old witch angrily. "Nonsense. They were mortals. One Halloween they stumbled upon my cottage and tried to eat it, tried to *eat* my house!" she cried. "Wouldn't you be mad if someone tried to eat *your* house?" she asked, turning in Fred's direction.

"Yes," he said, looking at Marnie, who shrugged.

"Of course you would." Rumora spat on the dirt floor. "But I never tried to eat them! Mark my words. I don't even eat meat. I'm vegetarian." The witch seemed nauseated at the very thought of a meal of humans.

"They went back to the mortal world and slandered me, spreading rumors that I locked them in a cage and threatened to cook them for dinner. Bah!" She spat again on the floor, then composed herself.

"It was a taste of my own medicine, I guess," she continued sorrowfully. "Since those mortals smeared my good name, I have vowed *never* to talk about another living creature behind his back again."

Marnie and Fred exchanged worried glances. "Just this once?" pleaded Marnie. "All we need is his real name."

"Never!" Rumora shouted.

"But Aggie said—"

Rumora cut off Fred. "Aggie Cromwell?"

"Yes," said Marnie carefully, not knowing if what she was about to say was a good thing or a bad thing in the strange, old witch's mind. "I'm her granddaughter."

"You're a Cromwell witch, you say?" asked Rumora warily.

"Yes."

Rumora considered this development silently. Then without saying a word, she rose and went to a pantry. She pulled out a huge, gleaming butcher knife.

For a second, Marnie and Fred's eyes grew wide with fright as the knife's metal glinted in the fire-light. But Rumora quickly cut down a bunch of hanging, dried herbs and abandoned the knife on a wooden table. She walked to the black cauldron in front of Fred and Marnie. Crumbling the dried herbs, which easily turned to powder in her bony hands, she sprinkled them into the pot. With a long wooden spoon, she began to slowly stir the bubbling liquid.

"Might you be interested in some soup?" she asked.

"No, thanks. We already ate," said Fred.

Rumora kept stirring. "I think you might like what's in it," she said quietly.

Marnie rose from her chair and peered over the side of the cauldron. She waved at Fred to join her. Inside, like alphabet soup, letters floated on the troubled surface of the brew. Slowly they combined to spell a word: Belial.

"Belial?" Marnie said aloud. Was Rumora telling them La Biel's real name was Belial?

"I told you nothing!" Rumora said sharply. The letters instantly disappeared, but Marnie smiled gratefully.

"Now, get me some bowls from the shelf," Rumora said. "You'll need nourishment for the long road ahead."

With a belly full of Rumora's surprisingly

delicious soup and the knowledge of La Biel's real name, Fred's courage was strengthened.

He and Marnie had hurried back from the witch's gingerbread cottage, making a quick stop to see Willow before heading to the edge of the forest and the bush where they'd hidden Marnie's broom.

Now, the two were flying high above Halloweentown, back to Witch University and Dylan. Fred tried not to look down as Marnie masterfully guided the broom over green fields and what looked like miniature villages.

Considering the day he had had, Fred felt emboldened. He had never ridden on a broom before. He had also never asked a girl on a date. Today was a day for firsts.

"Marnie," Fred started in a voice he hoped sounded confident. "I know maybe this isn't the *best* time, but there's something I've been meaning to ask you. When this is all over—I mean, when we get the amulet back and all—do you wanna grab a cup of coffee at Moonbucks? Like, with me?" he added, in case she thought he was just inquiring about her like or dislike for cappuccino.

Fred could feel his heart pounding in his chest as he waited for Marnie's answer.

"That's sweet, Fred. You're a really great scarecrow, but Ethan is actually my boyfriend," Marnie said. She turned and smiled gently back at Fred.

"Oh." Fred nodded. A slight blush crept up his embarrassed face. "Okay. Cool. I understand," he said. "No worries."

Marnie put her hand on top of Fred's on the broom. "But I couldn't have asked for a better detective partner," she continued. "Thank you for your help today."

Fred's blush deepened to a bright pink. "My pleasure," he smiled, meaning it.

CHAPTER
SEVEN

Marnie and Fred found Dylan still in his room, huddled over his precious magicbiology textbook.

"Restoratum memori edwyn por Belial!" Marnie shouted as she burst through the door.

"Why are you casting a remembering spell on me?" A confused Dylan looked up from his book. "And who's Belial? Fred, what are you doing here?" he asked, noticing his friend.

"Hey, dude," said Fred. "Can you tell us where the Gift is?"

"How do you know about the Gift?" asked Dylan, who looked quizzically at his sister.

"Dylan, can you remember where you hid it?" Marnie asked, crossing the room to take his arm. "It's important."

"Of course," said Dylan. Marnie and Fred sighed with relief. "But it's not here."

"Where is it, Dylan?" asked Marnie, a feeling of panic rising in her chest.

"I gave it to La Biel. He needs it for the youth serum."

"WHAT?!" Marnie and Fred both shouted at the same time.

"I know what you're gonna say." Dylan put his hands up defensively. "At first I didn't want to give it to him, either. I mean, it's the amulet! But then he explained it to me. In a slow, steady, rational voice—come to think of it. It almost put me to sleep the way he was talking. . . . Anyway, it all made sense."

"*How* did it make sense?" asked Marnie, squinting at her brother.

Dylan opened his mouth but was at a loss for words. "I can't really explain it now, but—"

"Dylan, you were hypnotized!" Marnie shouted.

"But this is *important* work, guys. LaBiel's discovery could change the world! Just imagine being able to turn back the clock on aging." Dylan had obviously bought into La Biel's hypnotic sales pitch hook, line, and sinker.

Marnie shook her head. "Dylan, if La Biel—Belial—has the Gift, he virtually rules Halloweentown. His intentions are not pure. Trust us."

"Why are you calling him Belial?" Dylan asked.

"Dude, he's not who he says he is. We have it on good authority," Fred explained.

"Then who is he?" asked Dylan nervously.

"We're not sure," Marnie said, sitting down at Dylan's computer, "but we're going to find out."

Marnie typed the word "Belial" in the search bar and hit "enter." She clicked on the first link.

Fred read over her shoulder: "'In the year 1042, a powerful demon named Azazel was wed to the witch Morgan Paganus. In 1287, they gave birth to their firstborn son, Belial. . . .'"

"So he's the son of a powerful demon and a witch," said Marnie, turning toward Dylan.

"Let me see," Dylan said, pushing Fred aside. He read out loud: "'In 1589, Belial was censured by the High Court of Magical Creaturedom for "unnatural acts" but disappeared before he could face punishment.'"

Dylan's face grew grey. "What do you think they mean by 'unnatural acts'?" he said. "Oh, no. I think I might have made a mistake."

"Can I get that on record?" asked a glum Marnie.

"So then what does he intend to do with the Gift?" asked Fred.

"And how do we get it back?" added Marnie.

The three sat in silence, pondering those two questions until Marnie shot up with a start.

"Sophie!" she remembered.

"What's wrong with Sophie?" inquired Dylan.

"Geez, you miss a lot when you dedicate your life to the pursuit of knowledge."

Marnie realized that they hadn't heard back from Grandma Aggie about whether their sister had been found. She flipped open her cellular witch's glass and said her grandmother's name. It rang a few times before Aggie's face appeared in the mirror. The picture was fuzzy and her voice distant and hard to hear over the static.

"Grandma, any luck finding Sophie?" Marnie asked hopefully.

"No, dear," Aggie said, shaking her head. "Not yet."

Now Marnie was worried. "Okay, I'm going to help you look for her."

"Excellent. I have a lead for you," said Aggie through the static. "I met a lovely fairy who told me she'd heard a young girl's voice coming from the eastern corner of the etherworld. Perhaps you could start searching there?"

"Copy, Grandma. Signing off," said Marnie, flipping her cell shut. "I'm going after Sophie.

You," she instructed Dylan and Fred, "figure out how to get the amulet from La Biel."

Marnie stood up straight and closed her eyes. Then, in a puff of golden smoke, she was gone.

CHAPTER
EIGHT

"Sooophie!" Marnie called, as if she were searching the neighborhood for a lost puppy. "Sooophie!"

Marnie had never been to this edge of the etherworld before. Pink-and-yellow–tinted fog churned at her feet and around her head, preventing her from seeing where she was going. In her ears, there was a high-pitched ringing noise, "the music of the spheres," Aggie had once explained. It was beautiful but disorienting.

Marnie stopped. Above the steady ringing, she

thought she heard something. The mists continued to swirl around her. Now she could definitely hear it: a girl's voice. She moved toward it.

"Sophie?" she called.

"Marnie?" the answer came back to her.

Marnie approached her reflection in a mirrored gateway. The gateway was large, almost twice as tall as Marnie, and framed in silver. Two ivory owls peered down at her from the top. The mirror rippled when Marnie touched it with her fingertips. Stepping through, she found herself in a dizzying hall of mirrors.

"Sophie?" she called again.

"I'm over here!" Sophie called back.

Marnie turned around and around, but everywhere she looked, her own reflection stared back at her. This place was like a funhouse!

"Follow my voice," Sophie called out. She started to sing a familiar lullaby their mother used to sing to them at bedtime.

Marnie closed her eyes and let her ears lead her

through the maze of mirrors. "Marnie!" she heard and suddenly felt herself being embraced. She opened her eyes to find Sophie hugging her.

"I thought you'd never find me! That crazy scientist locked me in here!"

Sophie wasn't alone. Next to her stood a girl about Marnie's age. In fact, she looked a lot like Marnie, only instead of jeans and a tank top, she wore a long, green velvet gown with gold lace trim. Her strawberry blond hair flowed down her back.

Sophie noticed her sister looking quizzically at her new friend. "Marnie, this is Maggie," she explained. "She's been trapped here for six hundred years!"

"Hi, Maggie," Marnie said, trying to figure out where she'd seen this girl before.

"Hello," Maggie said. She took Marnie's hand. "Thank you ever so much for coming to our aid. Sophie and I were mightily afraid we might never see the clear light of day again!" she exclaimed.

"Right," Marnie said, wondering why the girl talked in such a strange way. "Well, let's get you out of here."

"We've tried," lamented Sophie, "but this isn't a normal witch's glass."

"It's a hall of witch's glass," explained Maggie. "It's very strong. It requires the Power of Three to break out."

"Well, you're in luck," said Marnie, "'cause math may not be my best subject, but I do know two and one makes three!"

Marnie put her palms out beside her. Maggie and Sophie joined their palms with hers and with each other's, forming a Unity Circle. All three witches closed their eyes. The room trembled. Rainbows of light arced over, under, and around them. With a great ringing sound, like a clear bell, the mirrors shattered into a fine dust and blew away on a mighty wind that ruffled the witches' hair and clothes.

They opened their eyes. They were back in Halloweentown, in Marnie's dorm room. Fred,

Dylan, and Ethan were there to greet them. It felt like a party, as everyone took turns hugging Sophie—all except for Fred, who smiled at Sophie dumbly as he introduced himself—and meeting Maggie.

Only, Maggie no longer appeared as she had just moments ago. No aging can happen in a witch's glass, but freed from her prison, Maggie had been transformed into her real age. A few wrinkles lined her pretty, pale face, and her hair was shorter and swept up. Her body filled out the green dress differently. She looked strikingly similar, in fact, to Aggie.

Their likeness made Marnie remember. She sent a quick text message: "Got her!" and within seconds, Aggie shimmered into the room.

Aggie walked over and hugged her granddaughter tightly. "Sophie," she fussed, "we were so worried."

"I'm okay, Grandma," Sophie said. Her words were muffled against her grandmother's chest. She finally managed to pull away. "I want you to meet my friend. She was trapped with me in the witch's glass. This is—"

"—Maggie!" whispered an astonished Aggie.

"Splendora?" Maggie gasped.

They embraced as Marnie, Dylan, and Sophie exchanged confused glances.

"It's Aggie now," said their grandmother, wiping a tear from her eye. "What happened to you? We thought you'd run away to be with William!"

"Of course not. I could never have married him against my family's wishes," explained Maggie.

Aggie's eyes were wide with astonishment and relief. Remembering they had an audience, she turned to her grandkids.

"Marnie, Sophie, Dylan, I'd like you to meet your great-aunt—my sister—Margaret Juliet Cromwell."

"You have a sister?" asked an amazed Dylan.

"She disappeared ages ago . . ." said Aggie.

"Literally," confirmed Maggie.

"Our parents didn't approve of her boyfriend—he was a mortal . . ."

"Whatever happened to Billy?" Maggie asked, a wistful glimmer in her eye.

"He went on to write a bunch of plays, I believe. I even saw one at the Globe once. Very good, but could have used a few musical numbers if you'd asked me . . . But of course, Maggie had many other suitors as well."

"Yes, and one very angry one. Belial." Maggie's eyes narrowed when she said his name. "He was so incensed that I would scorn his love and choose a mortal over him, that he trapped me in the hall of mirrors."

"Did you say Belial?" repeated Marnie.

"Yes," Maggie said, surprised that Marnie knew the name.

"Grandma, Belial is La Biel," Marnie said excitedly. "Dylan, La Biel is Belial!"

"Of course!" exclaimed Aggie, bumping herself with the heel of her palm on her forehead. "I should have known! I knew I recognized him from somewhere. I hadn't seen him since he was banished by the Halloweentown Council, but he was just a young warlock then. He hasn't aged very well, if you ask me—all that crazy, gray hair." Aggie looked knowingly at Maggie. "I thought there was something dark about that man."

Suddenly, there was a knock at the door. Marnie pointed at it, and it creaked open. Stan entered the room. He was flustered and in a hurry.

"Sophie!" he exclaimed, a blush rising to connect the dots on his freckled face. "They found you!"

"Hi, Stan," Sophie said disinterestedly. "We're kind of in the middle of something here. Can you declare your love later?"

"Actually, I—I was looking for Ethan," he sputtered. "There's something going on at the research center. You'd better come quick!"

Dylan and Fred looked at each other. "La Biel," they said in unison. "We'll come with you, Stan," said Dylan. "I got us into this mess; I'll get us out."

At the door, Fred stopped. He had an idea. "Wait.

Let's take my skateboard. It'll get us there faster."

He pulled the skateboard from his backpack, and he and Dylan stepped on. It was a tight squeeze, but Fred skated off down the hall. Stan jogged after them.

"I'd better go with him," said Aggie anxiously. "He doesn't know what he's dealing with. You kids stay here." She snapped her fingers and then disappeared.

"I'm not missing this!" cried Sophie. "Besides, I want to show that mad professor he can't make a science experiment out of Sophie Piper," she said angrily, her hands on her hips.

"Wait, Sophie, it's not safe—" But before Marnie could stop her, Sophie had already snapped her fingers and disappeared, too.

"You know, I'd like to give that Belial a piece of my mind, as well," said Maggie, raising her hand to snap.

Marnie grabbed it. "Wait!" she cried. "La Biel—or Belial—whoever he is, must suspect we're coming. We should go in stealth mode."

CHAPTER NINE

An ominous black cloud hung over the Witch U. Research Center for Magical Science. The wind picked up, blowing furiously as Marnie, Ethan, and Maggie approached. Marnie was on her cell, trying to call Gwen.

"Still no answer," she said anxiously. "It's strange. She always has her witch's glass on . . . I guess we should go ahead." Marnie gazed nervously up at the massive Gothic stone building.

Silently they slid through the large front doors and tiptoed down the clean, white hallways. They came to a set of doors with frosted glass windows emblazoned with the words, CAUTION: Ongoing Magical Experimentation.

"Wait a second," whispered Marnie. She stuck out her arms, halting Ethan and Maggie in midstride.

"Anweledyn!" she said in a low voice, tapping each of them on the head with her pinky finger. "Now we're invisible," she smiled. "Ready?"

Maggie and Ethan nodded and Marnie pushed open the swinging doors. The hall before them was bright beneath the fluorescent lights.

They'd taken only three steps when, suddenly, they heard the sound of footsteps behind them. They turned in alarm. It was Stan. Ethan started to say something, but Marnie put her finger to his lips and shook her head. She didn't want to blow their cover. When Stan had unknowingly passed them, Marnie motioned to follow him.

Stan turned left when the hallway came to a fork and went through the open door, into the laboratory. Ethan, Marnie, and Maggie followed on his heels, cloaked in invisibility. Inside the lab were Sophie, Aggie, Dylan, Fred—and a smiling La Biel!

"Stanley," said the wild-eyed scientist, reaching out his hand.

Ethan moved as if to warn Stan, maybe pull him back from the warlock-demon's clutches, but Marnie and Maggie grabbed Ethan's arms.

"I believe you all know my nephew," said La Biel, putting his arm around Stan's shoulders.

"Nephew?" asked Sophie.

"Yes, of course." The professor smiled scornfully at her. "And now that we're all here—" He walked over to Aggie and caressed her face. He had clearly mistaken her for Maggie. "I guess we can get down to making history."

"You're not making anything but a big mistake, La Biel. We know who you are," said a defiant Dylan.

"Yes, I would hope my love would recognize me," La Biel said, looking at Aggie. "But you two," he pointed two long fingers at Fred and Dylan, "I've had about enough of . . ."

Instantly, Fred went inanimate. The smile on his face froze, and his arms sprung out stiffly by his sides. Dylan was gone and in his place was a black crow. He flew to Fred's shoulder and tried to protest, but all he could do was caw.

"Now you, my dears," La Biel said, turning his attention to Aggie and Sophie, "are probably wondering what this is all about."

They glared at him. They were wondering exactly that.

La Biel pulled the Gift from the pocket of his white lab coat. It glistened beneath the lab's bright lights. He held it before him, admiring it.

"With this amulet," said La Biel, "I'll finally get what I deserve—" Stan cleared his throat. "What *we* deserve," La Biel corrected himself.

"What no serum or potion or formula can give me—" Stan cleared his throat again. La Biel looked at him, annoyed. "Can give *us*." He paused for effect. "Your love."

Ceremoniously, La Biel lowered the amulet around his neck. It glowed a deep amber, infusing the room with energy. Immediately, Aggie and Sophie began to stare at La Biel and Stan like love-struck, obedient puppies. Marnie shivered as she watched helplessly and invisibly from the doorway.

"And with my youth serum, we shall live—the king and his queen. . . ." At this, Aggie slipped her arm through La Biel's.

"And the prince and his princess . . ." Sophie did the same to Stan.

"Shall live happily ever after, forever in their youthful states!" La Biel finished triumphantly.

Marnie and Maggie exchanged horrified looks. As the two couples whispered sweet nothings to each other and Dylan helplessly cawed, Marnie dragged Maggie and Ethan out the lab door and back into the hall.

"What are we going to do?" she groaned. "My grandmother and sister are under the power of the Gift; my brother is a crow; and my mother is nowhere to be found!" She realized, finally, that she was in over her invisible head.

"I wish I could help you," whispered Maggie regretfully, "but six hundred years in a hall of witch's glass has left my magic a bit rusty."

"I guess that scarecrow friend of yours can't help you now!" Ethan said, a little bitterly.

Marnie looked at him strangely. "Of course not, Ethan, he's a scarecrow!"

Ethan shrugged resentfully, and Marnie's face softened. She realized Ethan was jealous.

"Although, he *is* kind of cute," she said.

Ethan's eyes burned with jealousy, and his mouth hung open in shock. How could Marnie say such a thing? And in front of him?!

"Relax, Ethan! I'm kidding! *You're* my boyfriend. No one's as cute as you," she assured, hugging him around the waist.

"Do you mean that?" he asked, still pouting a little.

"Of course I do. But now's not the time for jealous boyfriends. Now is the time to get back the amulet and break Belial's hold on my family." She composed herself. "What are we going to do?"

"If only there was a way to get someone on the 'inside,' ya know? Like undercover," suggested Ethan.

"Normally I'd say you've watched too many cop shows, but this time I think you're on to something. Belial's obviously mistaken Grandma for you, Aunt Maggie," Marnie whispered. "What if we switch her for you?"

Ethan looked hopeful at the idea, but Maggie wasn't convinced. "How are we going to do that?" she asked.

"Magic?" Ethan offered.

"With the Gift, Belial's power is too strong. It's like a force field," said Maggie, shaking her head. "Everyday magic won't work in its presence, if it defies his purpose."

"We're gonna have to do it old-school," agreed Marnie.

CHAPTER
TEN

Marnie drummed her fingers against her chin, thinking. She peeked around the doorway into the lab. La Biel had a beaker filled with a cloudy liquid in his hand.

"The only thing missing," an impatient La Biel explained to Stan, "are the tears of a Cromwell witch in her thirteenth year. And your dear Sophie is a direct Cromwell descendent."

Turning, they both looked at Sophie, who blinked innocently back at her new beloved, Stan.

"Maggie, my darling," La Biel said in a smarmy

voice to the enraptured Aggie, "will you be a dear and get your love a fresh test tube from the storage closet?"

Aggie obediently headed for the doorway. Marnie popped back into the hallway.

"Now!" she whispered to Maggie.

Aggie, unaware of her invisible sister and granddaughter, opened the door to the closet. She hummed happily as she searched for the test tubes. Grabbing two, she turned to leave. Only the test tubes were unexpectedly plucked from her hands by the disguised Ethan. The door closed in her face.

"Sorry, Grandma," Marnie whispered through the door, over Aggie's muffled sounds of protest. "You'll thank me later."

"Okay, now remember," Marnie said, turning to Maggie. "You have to act like you're in love with him."

Maggie shuddered. "If I can successfully do that, then I deserve the lead role in one of William's plays."

"I can't promise that," said Marnie, "but we'll see about a Witch's Choice Award."

"My love, are you having trouble?" La Biel's voice called from inside the lab.

Maggie gave Marnie one last hopeful glance and bravely walked into the room. Marnie and Ethan huddled at the doorway, breathlessly watching to see if their body double would pass the test.

"Did you change clothes?" asked a surprised La Biel.

For a moment Maggie was speechless. Flustered, she looked down at her green velvet dress, quite different from the purple dress and red cape Aggie had been wearing just moments ago.

"You noticed?" she asked nervously. Then with more confidence, she continued, "Yes, I wanted something more appropriate for our triumphant moment. A witch likes to dress her best for her warlock."

Maggie batted her eyelashes and coyly sauntered up to La Biel's side, handing him one of the test tubes. He took it with a silly grin.

"Shall we get down to it?" he asked, tearing his attention away from Maggie.

La Biel turned his attention to Sophie. Stan had seated her on a stool in the center of the lab. "Ah, my dear," he said. "How are you feeling this afternoon?"

"Fine," said a dazed Sophie.

"Are you sure?" asked La Biel, circling her.

Stan watched, biting his fingernails.

"I think so," she stammered.

"You had a birthday recently, didn't you, Sophie?" La Biel was speaking in a low, hypnotic voice.

"Yes," Sophie answered.

"Are birthdays a painful time for you?"

"I don't think so," she said, confused.

"Even after that time your family *forgot* to celebrate your birthday?" he asked skeptically. "That would make me very sad, I think."

Sophie was silent, thinking back.

"That's not fair!" Marnie hissed to Ethan.

"That was right after Dad died. She said she didn't want to celebrate. She locked herself in her room, so we celebrated a week later!"

"He's just trying to make her cry, Marn," Ethan whispered.

Marnie glared at the professor.

"Wasn't that the year you got a puppy for Christmas?" La Biel inquired.

"Jeez! He's really done his research," Marnie grumbled quietly.

Sophie momentarily brightened. "Boo! I named him, 'Boo.'"

"The one that ran away?" La Biel pushed. "You never found him, did you, Sophie?"

Sophie's chin began to tremble, her smile dropping into a frown. She shook her head and looked down at her feet.

"This is too much," exclaimed Marnie. With a touch of her finger, her invisibility evaporated, and she ran to Sophie, taking her hand.

"Don't listen to what he says, Soph," she pleaded, looking into her bewildered younger sister's eyes. "He's just trying to make you cry, so he can use your tears for the serum. Don't cry, Sophie. Think of happy things."

Stan looked stunned at Marnie and Ethan's sudden and unexpected appearance, but La Biel didn't flinch.

"I thought you might choose to bless us with your presence, Marnie," he said. "Thank you for coming. You're just in time for the show. I'll make sure you have front-row seats."

La Biel raised his hand and snapped his fingers, and just as easily as opening or closing a door, he shrunk Marnie and Ethan to the size of mice and imprisoned them in one of the lab's many cages.

Ethan looked down at his new tiny size. "Uh-oh," he said, kicking the cedar shavings at his feet. "I hope they don't test on humans."

Marnie continued pleading with Sophie. She shouted from the cage with all the power she could muster from her mouse-size voice. "Sophie, remember happy things! Like the first time I took you trick-or-treating or . . . or how you felt when you cast your first spell!"

"Don't listen to her, Sophie," insisted Stan. He put his hand on her shoulder. "Listen to my uncle. He's going to help us stay young forever. Then you'll always be happy."

La Biel pushed him aside. "Thank you, Stanley. Sophie, think of all the sad things that have ever happened in your sad, little mortal life. It's been quite a pity, hasn't it, having to keep your powers under wraps for so long?"

"Don't cry!" shouted Marnie.

Suddenly, Dylan started squawking like crazy. "Caw! Caw, caaaaww!" he screeched.

Stan covered his ears and squinched up his freckled face.

"Caw! Caw, caw!" Dylan the crow continued. He was hopping up and down on Fred's frozen, extended arm.

"Shhhh! Dylan, I'm trying to help Sophie," Marnie called out. "Why is he squawking like that?" she asked Ethan.

"Wait . . ." Ethan motioned excitedly. "I think I know what he's saying."

"He's saying 'caw, caw, caw,'" said Marnie, rolling her eyes.

By now, Dylan was flapping wildly around the room. Stan was lunging after him, trying to grab the screeching black bird in his hands.

"CAAAWWW!" Dylan cried.

Stan pounced on him, knocking over a microscope, which clattered to the floor. He lifted his hands to discover Dylan was not under them, but was flying overhead.

"I've been sitting in on Animal Divination at the summer school," Ethan explained to Marnie. He was listening intently to Dylan's high-pitched shrieking.

"You can speak crow?" asked an incredulous Marnie.

"Kind of," he shrugged. "I gave up my magical powers, but I figured I could still learn a few sorcery tricks. Just for fun."

"So what is he saying?"

Dylan was flapping around, Stan poking at him with a broom he'd conjured.

"He says the serum calls for three—no two, definitely two—drops of tears. If we put in more, it may throw the magical reaction off."

Marnie looked at Ethan skeptically. "Are you sure?" she asked. "That's what he's saying?"

Ethan didn't look too positive, but he nodded. "Yes, I'm sure."

Finally, La Biel, tired by the commotion that was distracting Sophie from producing tears, pointed at Dylan. Instantly, the yapping crow turned into a paper crane. It floated slowly and silently to rest on Fred's head.

Marnie gasped. "Okay, he's turned my brother into origami. I guess it's our only shot." She turned to Sophie, who was looking attentively into La Biel's eyes. "Cry, Sophie! Think of the saddest thing you can remember!" she shouted.

"Come on, Soph. You can do it! Cry!" Ethan joined in. "Wait," he stopped, grabbing Marnie's arm to get her attention. "How are we going to get more tears into the serum?"

"Maggie," Marnie answered. She looked at her great-aunt, hoping her sense of drama was as keen as her grandmother's.

"Whoa is me!" Marnie bemoaned loudly. "There will surely be more tears before this day is out! *More* tears!"

Maggie glanced at the cage behind La Biel's back and winked, just as Sophie's chin began again to tremble.

"Here she goes," said Marnie. She crossed her fingers. "I've seen that face a hundred times."

CHAPTER ELEVEN

It started as a sniffle, then Sophie's eyes turned watery. La Biel held the beaker of cloudy serum below Sophie's chin. Two single tears sprang from Sophie's eyes, making a crystal trail down her cheeks and dropping into the serum. La Biel held the beaker up to his face, watching the tears swirl in the mixture as Sophie erupted into full-on sobs.

"There, there," said Maggie, going to comfort her niece. As she rubbed Sophie's back, she discreetly raised the second test tube beneath Sophie's chin, catching more of the salty tears.

"Darling," Maggie said to her evil suitor, "may I ask for just one kiss before we return to our younger selves."

Belial smiled a wicked smile. With one hand he held the beaker, with the other he smoothed his wiry, gray hair. As he leaned in for the kiss, Maggie quickly dumped her test tube of Sophie's tears into the beaker. At the last moment, she turned her face, offering her cheek rather than her lips.

"My love, your modesty ignites my desire even more," exclaimed an impassioned La Biel.

La Biel was unable to wait any longer. "Sophie, come join Stanley, your prince," he ordered.

A sniffling Sophie, her eyes swollen from crying, obediently took her place between Stan and La Biel. The scientist poured a thimbleful of the steaming liquid into the test tube.

"Together, on this day, we drink from the fount of youth!" he proclaimed.

Thunderclouds clapped outside the research center. The afternoon light glowed purple, and the lights inside the lab flickered.

La Biel triumphantly raised the test tube to his lips and threw it back, gulping the serum down before passing the glass tube to his nephew.

Marnie and Ethan clung to each other in the cage, breath held.

They didn't have to wait long. La Biel abruptly dropped to his knees, clutching his chest. Stan gasped. His uncle fell to the floor on all fours. The hair on his head shortened. It was retreating *back* into his head! The wrinkles and lines on his face smoothed over until his skin was perfect and pink. He began to shrink.

Within moments, what sat on the floor, gazing up at his "queen, prince, and princess," was not a man in the bloom of youth, but a baby! He sat on his naked bottom in the middle of a rumpled, white lab coat and sucked on the amulet that had formerly hung around the mad scientist's neck. It was Baby Belial!

Marnie and Ethan jumped up and down in the cage, hugging. Maggie swooped in and grabbed the Gift from Belial's mouth, wiping off the spit as the baby gurgled happily.

Just then, there was a commotion in the hall. All eyes turned to the lab door as Gwen appeared! She was out of breath and frantic.

"Sophie!" she cried, rushing to hug her youngest daughter. But Sophie, still under Belial's spell, looked confused. She shied away from her mother's touch.

"What's wrong, dear?" Gwen asked Sophie, alarmed. She looked to Maggie for an explanation, thinking her long-lost aunt was her mother.

"Oh!" cried Maggie with a glimmer in her eye. "I think I remember this one."

Maggie raised a ringed finger in the air and then pointed it at Sophie.

"Restoratum!" she said with confidence. The fog in Sophie's eyes dissipated. Maggie clapped at remembering the spell.

"Mom!" Sophie cried, hugging her mother before pulling back and continuing excitedly: "La

Biel turned Dylan into a crow and then a paper crane!"

Gwen turned to the odd scarecrow standing in the middle of the laboratory. "Restoratum!" she commanded.

Fred crumpled to the floor under the weight of Dylan, who was sitting on his head. They picked themselves up. Fred dusted himself off.

"Whoa, dude! That was one wicked spell!"

"Caw!" said Dylan. He cleared his throat. "I mean, yeah."

"Mom!" Marnie called from the cage. "Over here!" She struggled to be heard.

Gwen looked around, hearing her daughter's tiny voice.

"In the cage," said Stan sheepishly. Sophie glared at him.

Gwen opened the door to the cage, and Marnie and Ethan hopped onto her hand.

"Hi, honey," said a concerned Gwen, raising her miniature daughter up to eye level. "I'm sorry I couldn't get here earlier."

"I don't understand," said Marnie. "How did you even know to come at all? Your witch's glass was off."

Gwen smiled at Dylan. "A little bird told me. My cell was off because I was on the plane."

"I left her a message," explained Dylan. "I knew you wouldn't want to ask for help."

Marnie raised an eyebrow at her brother. He prepared for her complaint. "Thanks, Dyl," she said instead. "You know me better than I know myself." Looking down at her miniature body and then up at her mom, she added, "Now, can I return to that self?"

Gwen set Marnie and Ethan on the floor and closed her eyes. "Restoratum!"

They sprang back to normal size.

Sophie ran back to her mother's side and tugged on her hand. "Mom, they made me fall in love with Stan and Grandma with that crazy scientist!" she said excitedly. She was talking a mile a minute.

"Aggie!" said Ethan and Maggie.

"Grandma!" Marnie exclaimed at the same time.

"What's wrong? She's right here!" Gwen said, looking at Maggie.

"Well, not exactly," said Marnie. "I kind of locked her in the closet . . ."

"*You locked your grandmother in a closet?!*" Gwen shot Marnie a look that said she was in big trouble. Then, shaking her head, she glanced suspiciously at Maggie, who smiled back at her. "Then who's . . ."

Gwen was interrupted by her real mother's entrance into the lab. Aggie followed Ethan, who'd liberated her from the storage closet and quickly explained La Biel's wicked plan.

"Marnie, I never thought I'd say this," Aggie said, smoothing her skirts and hair, "but *thank you* for locking me in a closet!"

Gwen was now really perplexed. She looked back and forth between Aggie and Maggie. "Mother?" she asked.

"Yes, dear," reassured Aggie, taking her

hand. "I'd like you to meet Maggie."

"Your sister?" Gwen asked in amazement. "But I thought she . . ."

"Ran away with a mortal?" asked a smiling Maggie.

"Yes," answered Gwen. That was part of the reason her mother had been so opposed to her own marriage to a mortal. Aggie had been afraid of losing her sister *and* her daughter.

"Alas, that was not the case," said Maggie. "I was imprisoned."

"Oh," said Gwen, still befuddled by her mother's look-alike standing before her.

"Wait just one second there, Stanley!" Sophie suddenly shouted.

Stan had been edging silently toward the door of the lab. Hearing his name, he turned, caught like a deer in headlights.

"You're not going anywhere," she warned.

Stan bolted, running out the door.

"Hey!" cried Sophie.

"Pater Tiempo, grant us this spell, that we may

use your power well. Your never-ending nature we know, and ask your help to change the flow. Erwind temperatum temporalis," Aggie chanted.

Stan backpedaled into the room.

"You're not going anywhere," Sophie said again.

Aggie pointed her wand at the unfortunate Stan. A giant playpen sprung up around him and his baby uncle.

"This should keep you out of trouble until the Halloweentown Council can decide what to do with you," said Aggie.

"I have a feeling you're gonna be babysitting for a loooong time," joked Sophie.

Everyone laughed, especially Fred.

Maggie walked over to Marnie. "In the meantime, I think you should be the one to hold on to this," she said, handing the Gift back to Marnie.

"Just make sure you find a better hiding place this time!" said Gwen with a parental I-told-you-so look on her face.

"Hey!" cried Dylan, faking insult.

Gwen put her arm around her son's shoulders. "No offense," she smiled.

"None taken. Let's go home. I think I've had enough mad science for one day."

"Agreed," they all chimed in unison.

CHAPTER
TWELVE

"Guys, gals, and ghouls, without further ado," said Professor Periwinkle, the master of ceremonies for Witch University's Summer Sorcery School graduation, "I give you our class of 2007!"

With that, the crowd of young witches and warlocks seated in the university auditorium tossed up a hundred pointy, black witch's hats. They didn't wear them in real life, of course, but the symbolic effect was nice. And after three months of intensive studies in all things paranormal and magical, they figured they deserved a little bit of celebration. The university's marching band struck up a triumphant tune.

The Piper-Cromwell clan, accompanied by Ethan and Fred, was seated front row center. They clapped louder than anyone else. Sophie spotted them and waved, smiling proudly as she followed Stephanie, Sylvie, and the rest of the graduates out of the auditorium.

Marnie dabbed at a tear in the corner of her eye. Ethan, seated beside her, noticed.

"What's wrong?" he asked, alarmed.

"Oh, nothing." Marnie heaved a big sigh. "It's a sister thing. I just never thought I'd see Sophie grow up. She's a young witch now."

Gwen looked over and patted her daughter's leg.

Marnie wiped away another tear. "They grow up so fast!" she said, genuinely amazed.

"Welcome to my world," Gwen smiled.

Outside the auditorium, Marnie and Ethan sat apart from the rest of the family on a stone bench. Ethan rubbed Marnie's back.

"You okay now?" he asked. "With your 'sister thing'?"

Marnie laughed. "Yeah, I'll be okay." She smiled at him. "How are you?"

"I'm great," he said, shooting her a toothpaste-commercial smile.

"What are you so smiley about?" she teased. Marnie wiped some stray blond bangs out of Ethan's eyes.

"Listen, Marnie, I'm sorry that I got so jealous about Fred before . . ."

"I know," Marnie said, looking into Ethan's eyes. "You don't need to apologize."

"But I think I know why I did," he continued. He took her hand. "Marnie, I love you."

Marnie was speechless. Had Ethan just said "I love you," or was she hearing things?

"Well," he said expectantly, "are you gonna say anything?"

Ethan looked nervous. He shifted in his seat and looked earnestly at Marnie.

"I love you, too!" she blurted.

"Really?" he asked. "Or are you just saying it because I did?"

"No," said Marnie. The truth was, she had been falling in love with Ethan for a while now. He made her happy, happier than she'd ever been. And she trusted him. "I mean it."

Ethan smiled and leaned in for a kiss. He was two inches from Marnie's lips when a shadow descended upon them. They both turned their heads to look up. Sophie stood in front of them.

"Sorry to interrupt your Schmoopy-fest, but we're heading to Grandma's."

"Okay," Marnie sighed. "I'll meet you guys there. I just have one thing I need to do first."

"Suit yourself, but don't be late for dinner," said Sophie, turning on her heel.

"Hey, Sophie," Marnie called after her.

"Yeah?" Sophie turned.

"Good job. I'm proud of you."

A smile spread across Sophie's face. She glowed. "Thanks."

Marnie knocked three times on the cottage door and waited. The Gift weighed in her pocket like a heavy burden. She was ready to hide it again.

Marnie knew the old witch was home because smoke poured out of the chimney. She heard the pig oinking inside and Rumora mumbling something about people wanting to eat her out of house and home. Finally, the door creaked open.

"Yes?" said the old, blind witch. She was even more stooped over than Marnie remembered.

"It's me, Marnie Piper. Aggie's granddaughter."

Marnie thought she saw the hint of a smile cross the old woman's face. With one gnarled hand, she supported herself on a wooden cane. With the other, she felt Marnie's face and finally her hands.

"So it is. What can an old woman like me do for a young witch like you?" she croaked.

"Can you keep a secret?" Marnie asked.

Now there was no doubt Rumora was smiling.

Her crooked grin revealed two missing teeth.

"To the grave," she answered.

Aggie and Maggie sat at the ends of the long, wooden table. Between them, the chairs were full of family and friends, and the table was full of food. Steam spilled from full goblets, and serving platters of roast meat and bowls of mashed potatoes floated through the air, as everyone helped themselves to the celebratory feast.

In the middle sat the witch of the hour, Sophie. Everyone could see the bright smile on the happy graduate's face. What they couldn't see was that Sophie held Fred's hand under the table.

"Soph, there's something I've been meaning to ask you," Marnie said from across the table. "At the laboratory, what did you think about when we told you to be sad?"

Sophie smiled a sad smile. "Dad," she said.

Fred squeezed her hand under the table.

Marnie nodded. "And what did you think about when we told you to be happy?" she asked.

Sophie took a sip of hot cider as they waited for her answer. Finally, she smiled again. "Dad."

Gwen started to get teary. She got up from the table and went to stand behind Marnie and Dylan. She hugged their heads to her chest.

"Oh, my babies!" she said. She kissed each of them on top of the head.

"Mom . . ." Dylan started to say, but his objection to her physical displays of affection was drowned out by the sound of a car horn honking.

Gwen and Aggie looked at each other. Who could it be? They weren't expecting any more guests.

Aggie went to open the door, as everyone else raced to the window, josting to see who it was.

Benny's yellow cab idled outside Aggie's house. He tipped his hat.

"Sorry to interrupt your celebration, folks, but I'm under orders to bring the Cromwell witches to City Hall."

"But why?" asked a surprised Aggie.

"Emergency meeting of the Halloweentown

Council," Benny whispered. Inside the house, Marnie and Gwen looked at each other.

"Don't tell 'em I told ya," Benny said, "but there's trouble with the portal."

Disney
HIGH SCHOOL MUSICAL 2

Coming Soon To  And Disney DVD

HighSchoolMusicalDVD.com

Your music. Your way.

Now, there are five fun ways to listen to Radio Disney!

1) *On Your Radio...*
Go to RadioDisney.com to find your station

2) *On Your Computer...*
Stream Radio Disney LIVE on RadioDisney.com or on iTunes (Radio Area: Top 40/Pop)

3) *On Your TV...*
Via DirectTV's XM music channel

4) *On Satellite Radio...*
Go to Channel 115 on XM or Sirius satellite radio

5) *On Your Mobile Phone...*
Listen to Sprint Radio (Sprint) and MobiRadio (Cingular)

RadioDisney.com

©Disney